BEGINNER READER

RAINBOW magic ™

A Magical Birthday Surprise

Orchard Beginner Readers are specially created to develop literacy skills, confidence and a love of reading.

ORCHARD BOOKS

First published as "The Fairies' Birthday Surprise" in the USA in 2010 by Scholastic Inc
First published in Great Britain in 2015 by Orchard Books
This edition published in 2016 by The Watts Publishing Group

5 7 9 10 8 6 4

A CIP catalogue record for this book is available from the British Library.

ISBN 978 1 40833 680 9

Printed in China

The paper and board used in this book are made from wood from responsible sources

Orchard Books
An imprint of Hachette Children's Group
Part of The Watts Publishing Group Limited
Carmelite House, 50 Victoria Embankment, London EC4Y 0DZ

An Hachette UK Company
www.hachette.co.uk
www.hachettechildrens.co.uk

RAINBOW magic™

A Magical Birthday Surprise

Daisy Meadows

ORCHARD

A trumpet sounds from the Fairyland
Palace, and the Rainbow Fairies wake up.

"Is that the royal trumpet?" Ruby asks.
"Yes, today is the fairy queen's
birthday!" Sky remembers.
"We should do something special for her,"
Fern says.

"Let's bake her a cake," Izzy says.
"Yes," Saffron agrees. "Let's make it
from scratch."
"What does that mean?" Heather asks.

"It means we'll make it by hand," Saffron
explains, "and we won't use magic."
The fairy sisters look at each other.
They *always* use magic.

"Making it from scratch is special," Ruby says.
"Let's do it!"
Amber opens a cookbook.
"The recipe calls for sugar, butter, eggs, flour,
baking powder and milk," she reads aloud.
"We don't have eggs, milk or butter," she says,
looking up.

"I can make them!" Heather suggests, raising her wand.
"Wait!" declares Saffron. "We all agreed, no magic."

The Rainbow Fairies fly to the Fairyland farm. Ruby, Amber and Izzy head into the henhouse.

"Cluckity cluck," the hens call as the
fairies take eggs from their warm nests.
"Thank you, ladies," Izzy says as they leave.

The other fairies are in the cow barn.
"The recipe calls for milk and butter," remembers Fern.

"We can churn the milk into butter,"
Heather says.
Sky and Saffron sit down on the stools and
begin to milk the cow.

The fairies put the eggs and milk in a wagon, and Saffron pulls it along.
"This is hard work!" she says.
"It would be easier with magic," says Heather.

"But we agreed," Izzy insists.
"I know," answers Heather, "no magic."

The fairies return to the cottage.
Ruby and Amber crack the eggs.

Saffron and Fern churn the butter.
Sky, Izzy and Heather stir the mixture.
It is messy work!

The fairies pour the mixture into seven pans and put them in the oven.

Amber looks at the clock. "The cakes should be done just in time for the party," she says. "We'll wash up while they bake," says Saffron.

Ding!
"They are ready!" Fern declares.
Each fairy pulls a cake from the oven.

They stack the seven cakes and admire their hard work.

"Oh, no!" cries Saffron. "We forgot the icing."

"We don't have time to make icing from scratch," Amber says.
"We worked so hard," Ruby says. "A little magic couldn't hurt."

Sparkles whirl from Ruby's wand and swirl
around the cake.
At once, the cake is covered with white icing!
"Now we need to add colour," says Ruby.

But the fairies cannot agree on how to
decorate the cake.
Fern says, "The bottom layer should be green,
like grass." She flicks her wand, and green
icing covers the bottom cake.
"No, it should be blue," insists Sky.

All of the fairies want to make the cake
pretty, and each fairy has her own
favourite colour.
They all point their wands at the cake at the
same time.
Whoosh! Sparkles spin around the kitchen.

"What's happening?" asks Sky. "The sparkles won't stop."

"Maybe we used too much magic," Izzy suggests.

When the sparkles disappear, the fairies gasp. The cake is a mess of different colours.

"What should we do?" Saffron asks. "The party is starting."

"I don't think we should use any more magic," Amber says.

"We baked a cake for the queen," says Izzy. "We should give it to her."

The fairy sisters put the cake in their wagon and pull it to the royal garden.
The party has started, but the crowd grows quiet as the Rainbow Fairies wheel in the cake.
The king and queen smile at them.

"You baked me a cake!" says the fairy queen.
Amber cuts a piece and hands it to the queen.

The queen takes a bite. "It's delicious!" she exclaims. "It reminds me of my birthday cakes as a little fairy. My mother and I made them from scratch." She takes another bite.

"Except for the icing. We used a little magic for that." The queen smiles at the sisters. "I love the colourful icing. Only the Rainbow Fairies could have made this cake! It's a real treat."

When they have finished serving the guests, the Rainbow Fairies sit down to have some cake, too. "It's wonderful," says Amber.

"It is yummy," Heather agrees, "but my piece needs more icing." She gives her wand a twirl and a big violet icing flower appears.
"Yum!" she exclaims. "Now it tastes magical!"